Fluttersh...

FLUTTERSHY IS A KIND AND GENTLE PONY WITH BIG HEART. SHE LIKES TO TAKE CARE OF OTHERS, ESPECIALLY HER LITTLE ANIMAL FRIENDS.

D0972874

Rarity

RARITY KNOWS HOW TO ADD SPARKLE TO ANY OUTFIT! SHE LOVES TO GIVE HER PONY FRIENDS ADVICE ON THE LATEST FASHIONS AND HAIRSTYLES.

Rainbow Dash

RAINBOW DASH LOVES TO FLY AS FAST AS SHE CAN! SHE IS ALWAYS READY TO PLAY A GAME, GO ON AN ADVENTURE, OR HELP OUT ONE OF HER PONY FRIENDS.

Starlight Glimmer

STARLIGHT GLIMMER IS A POWERFUL UNICORN, AND TWILIGHT SPARKLE'S PUPIL. ONCE CONVINCED THAT PONIES SHOULD SURRENDER THEIR CUTIE MARKS TO IMPROVE FRIENDSHIP, HER ADVENTURES WITH TWILIGHT HAVE TAUGHT HER OTHERWISE.

Pinkie Pie

PINKIE PIE KEEPS HER
PONY FRIENDS LAUGHING
AND SMILING ALL DAY!
CHEERFUL AND PLAYFUL,
SHE ALWAYS LOOKS ON
THE BRIGHT SIDE.

Trixie

TRIXIE, OFTEN REFERRED
TO AS "THE GREAT AND
POWERFUL TRIXIE," IS A
TRAVELING MAGICIAN WHO'S
KNOWN FOR HER BOASTFUL
ATTITUDE AND HIT-OR-MISS
ILLUSIONS. SHE'S ALSO
STARLIGHT'S BEST FRIEND.

Celestial Advice

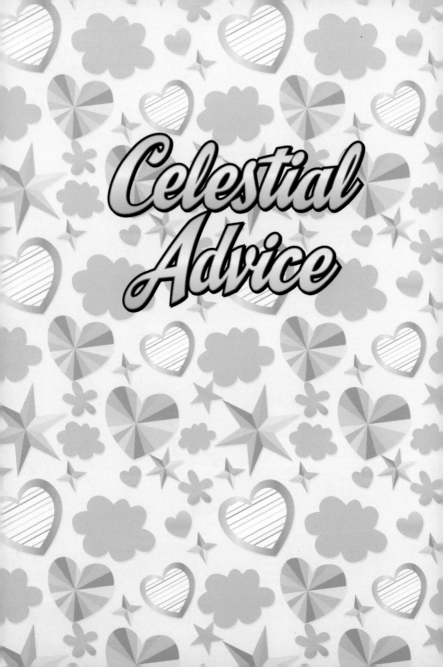

my LiTTLE PONY
Star Pupil

Special thanks to Tayla Reo, Ed Lane,
Beth Artale, and Michael Kelly.

ISBN: 978-1-68405-495-4
22 21 20 19   1 2 3 4

Chris Ryall, President & Publisher/CCO
John Barber, Editor-in-Chief
Cara Morrison, Chief Financial Officer
Matthew Ruzicka, Chief Accounting Officer
David Hedgecock, Associate Publisher
Jerry Bennington, VP of New Product Development
Lorelei Bunjes, VP of Digital Services
Justin Eisinger, Editorial Director, Graphic Novels & Collections
Eric Moss, Sr. Director, Licensing & Business Development

Ted Adams and Robbie Robbins, IDW Founders

Licensed By:

www.IDWPUBLISHING.com

STAR PUPIL

Story by
Kristine Songco
and
Joanna Lewis

Adaptation by
Justin Eisinger

Edits by
Alonzo Simon

Lettering and Design by
Tom B. Long

MEET THE PONIES

Twilight Sparkle

TWILIGHT SPARKLE TRIES TO FIND THE ANSWER TO EVERY QUESTION! WHETHER STUDYING A BOOK OR SPENDING TIME WITH PONY FRIENDS, SHE ALWAYS LEARNS SOMETHING NEW!

Spike

SPIKE IS TWILIGHT SPARKLE'S BEST FRIEND AND NUMBER ONE ASSISTANT. HIS FIRE BREATH CAN DELIVER SCROLLS DIRECTLY TO PRINCESS CELESTIA!

Applejack

APPLEJACK IS HONEST, FRIENDLY AND SWEET TO THE CORE! SHE LOVES TO BE OUTSIDE, AND HER PONY FRIENDS KNOW THEY CAN ALWAYS COUNT ON HER.

KNOCK KNOCK

VRRRNNNN

OH, HEY SPIKE...

WHAT'S UP?

JUST, UH, WANTED TO MAKE SURE YOU'RE READY...

...FOR YOUR BIG CEREMONY TODAY.

VORT

YUP.

I STILL CAN'T BELIEVE MY FRIENDS AND I ARE GETTING MEDALS OF HONOR.

ARE YOU KIDDING? YOU TOTALLY DESERVE IT!

AFTER ALL, YOU SAVED EQUESTRIA... FROM QUEEN CHRYSALIS...

...WITH THE HELP OF TRIXIE, THORAX, AND DISCORD...

SPIKE'S JUST STALLING!

UM, YEAH. I KNOW WHAT HAPPENED. I WAS KINDA THERE.

VRRRNNN

RIGHT. UH, SO WHAT ARE YOU WEARING?

NOT SURE.

WHY, AM I SUPPOSED TO DRESS UP?

NO!

NO. I MEAN, YOU COULD.

IT'S LIKE RARITY ALWAYS SAYS...

"There's no such thing as overdressed.

"You're just the best-looking pony in the room!"

SPIKE CRANES HIS NECK TO SEE IF TWILIGHT IS ALL CLEAR.

WHAT ARE YOU LOOKING AT?

NO!

FWAP

DON'T LOOK!

JUST THEN, TWILIGHT GIVES THE SIGNAL...

...AND IS GONE IN A FLASH.

VORT

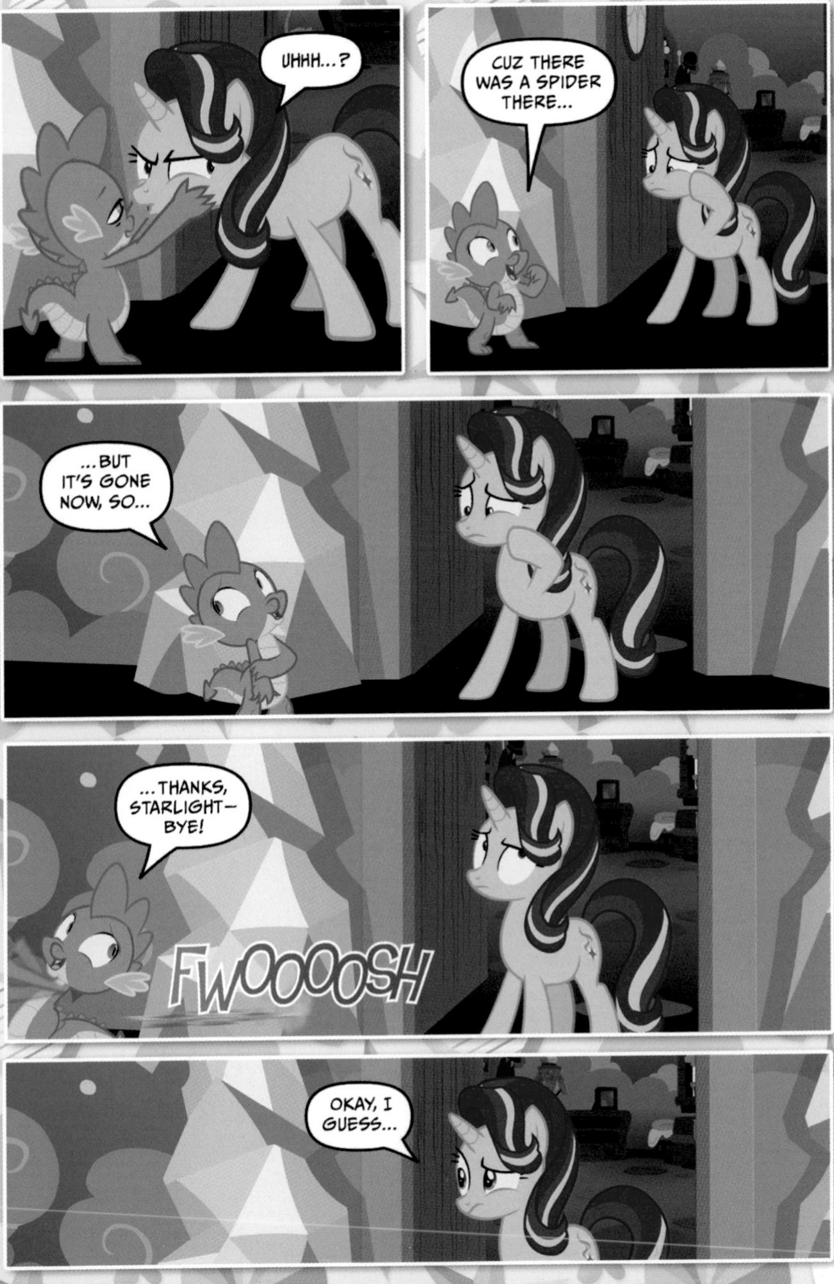
UHHH...?
CUZ THERE WAS A SPIDER THERE...
...BUT IT'S GONE NOW, SO...
...THANKS, STARLIGHT—BYE!
FWOOOOOSH
OKAY, I GUESS...

ELSEWHERE IN THE CASTLE...

VRRRNNN

BWUMP

HEH HEH. SHE HAD NO IDEA.

WE'RE A GOOD TEAM, SPARKLE.

SPARKLE? TEE-HEE...

YEAH WE ARE.

BUT DO YOU THINK SHE'LL LIKE IT?

I WANT THIS PRESENT TO SAY...

"I'M SO PROUD OF YOU, BOTH AS A MENTOR AND A FRIEND.

"EQUESTRIA IS SAFER THANKS TO YOU."

WHAT DO YOU THINK?

OH.

I THOUGHT YOU WERE GETTING HER A MIRROR—

—LIKE YOURS.

I AM!

MAYBE YOU SHOULD GET HER A CARD...

...CUZ I DON'T THINK THE MIRROR WILL SAY ALL THAT.

BUT I THINK SHE'LL LIKE IT.

IT'S JUST WHAT HER ROOM NEEDS.

THE FIRST THING SHE'LL SEE WHEN SHE WAKES UP...

...IS HERSELF SURROUNDED BY ALL HER FRIENDS!

I PLAN ON GIVING IT TO HER AFTER THE CEREMONY.

ABOUT THAT.

DON'T YOU NEED TO GET THE CASTLE READY FOR THE CELEBRATION?

NAH. PINKIE PIE'S GOT THAT COVERED.

MEANWHILE...

HMPH.

YOINK

BWOOOOSH

PHEW! THAT WAS TOUGH.

A SHORT WHILE LATER...

...STARLIGHT, TRIXIE, THORAX, AND DISCORD WERE BRAVE IN THE FACE OF DANGER.

RESOURCEFUL WHEN THINGS GOT CHALLENGING.

AND PROVED THAT THE BONDS OF FRIENDSHIP...

...NO MATTER HOW UNLIKELY...

...ARE STRONGER THAN ANY ADVERSITY.

BY STOPPING QUEEN CHRYSALIS, NOT ONLY DID THEY SAVE EQUESTRIA...

...THEY SET THE CHANGELINGS FREE FROM HER REIGN.

GO DISCORD! YA-HOO!

HEE-HEE.

THAT'S WHY WE'RE PROUD...

...AND HONORED TO GIVE THEM...

...THE EQUESTRIAN PINK HEARTS OF COURAGE.

Hooray! Ya-hoo!

EVERYONE BOWS TO RECEIVE THEIR MEDAL.

YEAH!!

WE ARE SO PROUD OF YOU ALL.

YAY! Way to go! You did it!

WE REALLY DID IT.

TOGETHER.

WHAT'S ON TWILIGHT'S MIND?

20

WUMP ♪ ♫ VP WUMP ♪ VP ♪

AT THE RECEPTION...

...EVERYPONY GETS TO CUT LOOSE.

IT WAS THE *GREAT* AND *POWERFUL* TRIXIE'S PLEASURE...

...TO SAVE YOU FROM YOUR *IMMINENT DOOM.*

SHWINK

YES. BECAUSE YOU DID IT ALL BY YOURSELF.

I CAN'T BELIEVE YOU MANAGED TO DO IT WITHOUT MAGIC.

IT WAS AMAZING!

NO ONE'S EVER STOOD UP TO CHRYSALIS LIKE THAT.

OH, I JUST DID...

...WHAT ANYPONY WOULD HAVE DONE.

IT'S A WONDERFUL FEELING, ISN'T IT?

WATCHING YOUR STUDENT SHINE THE WAY YOU ALWAYS KNEW SHE COULD.

MY CHEEKS ARE SORE.

I DON'T THINK I'VE EVER SMILED THIS MUCH IN MY LIFE.

I CAN ONLY IMAGINE WHAT THAT FEELS LIKE.

WINK

AS CELESTIA WANDERS OFF...

23

FAWHIP

YES, STARLIGHT IS STUDENT OF THE YEAR, ISN'T SHE?

SHE HAS SO MUCH POTENTIAL.

SO, WHAT ARE **WE** GOING TO DO WITH HER?

AND BY **"WE"** I DEFINITELY MEAN **YOU.**

DOINK

BEING HER MENTOR AND ALL...

...HER DESTINY FALLS **SQUARELY** ON YOUR SHOULDERS.

YORT

VIP

OH DON'T YOU WORRY.

I'VE PLANNED ENOUGH FRIENDSHIP LESSONS TO COVER THE NEXT THREE YEARS.

HAHA HAHA HA!

TWILIGHT WAS NOT READY FOR THAT!

WHAT'S SO FUNNY?

CLEARLY STARLIGHT IS BEYOND BASIC FRIENDSHIP LESSONS.

SHE JUST WON A *MEDAL,* FOR *EQUESTRIA'S* SAKE!

I THOUGHT YOU WERE JOKING.

YOINK

YOU ARE JOKING, RIGHT?

HA HA... OF COURSE I WAS.

OBVIOUSLY YOU SHOULD HAVE A GRANDIOSE, MASTER PLAN FOR HER...

...THE SAME WAY PRINCESS CELESTIA SET YOU ON A PATH...

...THAT EVENTUALLY MADE YOU A PRINCESS.

YUP!

OH GOOD.

I'M SURE SHE CAN'T WAIT TO HEAR ALL ABOUT IT!

OH NO!

SO HOW'S THE WHOLE *RULING-A-KINGDOM* THING GOING?

IT'S A BIT... OVERWHELMING. BUT WE'RE ADJUSTING.

OH STARLIGHT!

PRINCESS TWILIGHT HAS SOMETHING VERY IMPORTANT TO TELL US.

WELL, JUST YOU REALLY...

...BUT I'M *NOSEY* AND WANT TO HEAR.

OKAY, WOULD YOU—

VORT

—NEVERMIND.

WHAT'S GOING ON?

WELL!

TWILIGHT WAS JUST ABOUT TO REVEAL HER *BIG MASTER PLAN* FOR YOU.

REALLY?

I WAS KIND OF WONDERING WHAT WE WERE GOING TO DO NEXT...

YES, I'D SAY WE'RE BOTH FAIRLY INTERESTED.

OF COURSE YOU ARE. AND I DO HAVE A PLAN, OBVIOUSLY, BUT NOW'S CLEARLY NOT THE TIME TO DO IT.

STARLIGHT!

COME ON! THE *PONYVILLE CHRONICLE* WANTS TO TAKE OUR PICTURE!

UGH. YOU TOO, DISCORD.

TWILIGHT IS RELIEVED!

IT'S A TINY DISCORD!

PSST. I SEE WHAT YOU'RE DOING.

YOU DO?!

YES.

YOU ALREADY PLANNED THE PERFECT MOMENT DURING THE PARTY...

...TO MAKE A GRAND ANNOUNCEMENT TO *EVERYPONY* ABOUT YOUR PLAN!

VORT

BRAVA, TWILIGHT. I CAN'T WAIT TO TELL FLUTTERSHY AND THE OTHERS!

DISCORD, NO!

VIP

WITH DISCORD GONE, TWILIGHT RUNS FOR THE DOOR.

Clop Clop

CATCHING SPIKE'S ATTENTION AS SHE SLAMS THE DOOR BEHIND HER.

32

TWILIGHT? ARE YOU READING DURING A PARTY AGAIN?

CRINKLE

OH!

NO, NO, NO! SHE'S ALREADY GOOD AT THAT.

SHE MASTERED THIS.

SHE TAUGHT *ME* ABOUT THIS ONE!

WILD GUESS— SOMETHING'S WRONG.

SPIKE, I'M A TERRIBLE MENTOR.

WHY DIDN'T I COME UP WITH A PATH FOR STARLIGHT?

PRINCESS CELESTIA HAD IT ALL FIGURED OUT FOR ME—

GAH!

THAT'S IT!

BOING

COME ON!

IN TWILIGHT'S THRONE ROOM.

I HAD *YEARS* WORTH OF FRIENDSHIP LESSONS READY TO GO...

...BUT WHEN WE WERE CAPTURED BY CHRYSALIS...

...STARLIGHT TOOK CHARGE AND REALLY STEPPED UP.

I DON'T THINK FRIENDSHIP LESSONS ARE ENOUGH FOR HER ANYMORE.

SO YOU HAVE AN *OVER-ACHIEVING* STUDENT?

SOUNDS FAMILIAR.

THAT'S WHY I HAD TO TALK TO YOU.

YOU OF ALL PONIES WOULD KNOW WHAT TO DO.

I MEAN, YOU WERE ME AND I WAS STARLIGHT.

BUT FOR NOW, I NEED YOU TO PRETEND YOU'RE YOU AND I'M *ME*.

GO ON.

WHEN I WAS YOUR STUDENT AND YOU WERE IN THIS PLACE, YOU...

OH NO!

YOU SENT ME TO PONYVILLE.

WHICH MEANS, IT'S TIME FOR ME TO SEND *STARLIGHT GLIMMER* AWAY!

I CAN'T BELIEVE IT.

IT REALLY IS TIME FOR STARLIGHT TO GO, ISN'T IT?

ONLY YOU CAN MAKE THAT DECISION.

IT'S A DIFFICULT ONE...

...BUT YOUR HEART KNOWS WHAT'S RIGHT.

EVEN AS IT HURTS.

WHERE ARE YOU GOING TO SEND HER?

EEEE—!

SPIKE...

TOO SOON?

NO. THIS IS SOMETHING I HAVE TO DO.

TWILIGHT TAKES A LONG LOOK AT HER MAP.

OH BOY.

MEANWHILE, IN THE DINING HALL...

OH BOY.

...DISCORD IS SPINNING HIS MISCHIEVOUS YARNS.

I KNOW!

WHATEVER TWILIGHT'S PLANNING FOR STARLIGHT...

...IS GOING TO BE *SO EXCITING!*

WONDER WHY SHE DIDN'T TELL ANY OF US ABOUT IT?

PROBABLY BECAUSE YOU'RE NOT AS CLOSE AS YOU THINK YOU ARE.

JUST KIDDING!

SHE WANTED IT TO BE A SURPRISE.

JUST BETWEEN US, SHE'S GETTING READY TO MAKE A BIG ANNOUNCEMENT!

YEEEEEEE!

THAT'S SO EXCITING!

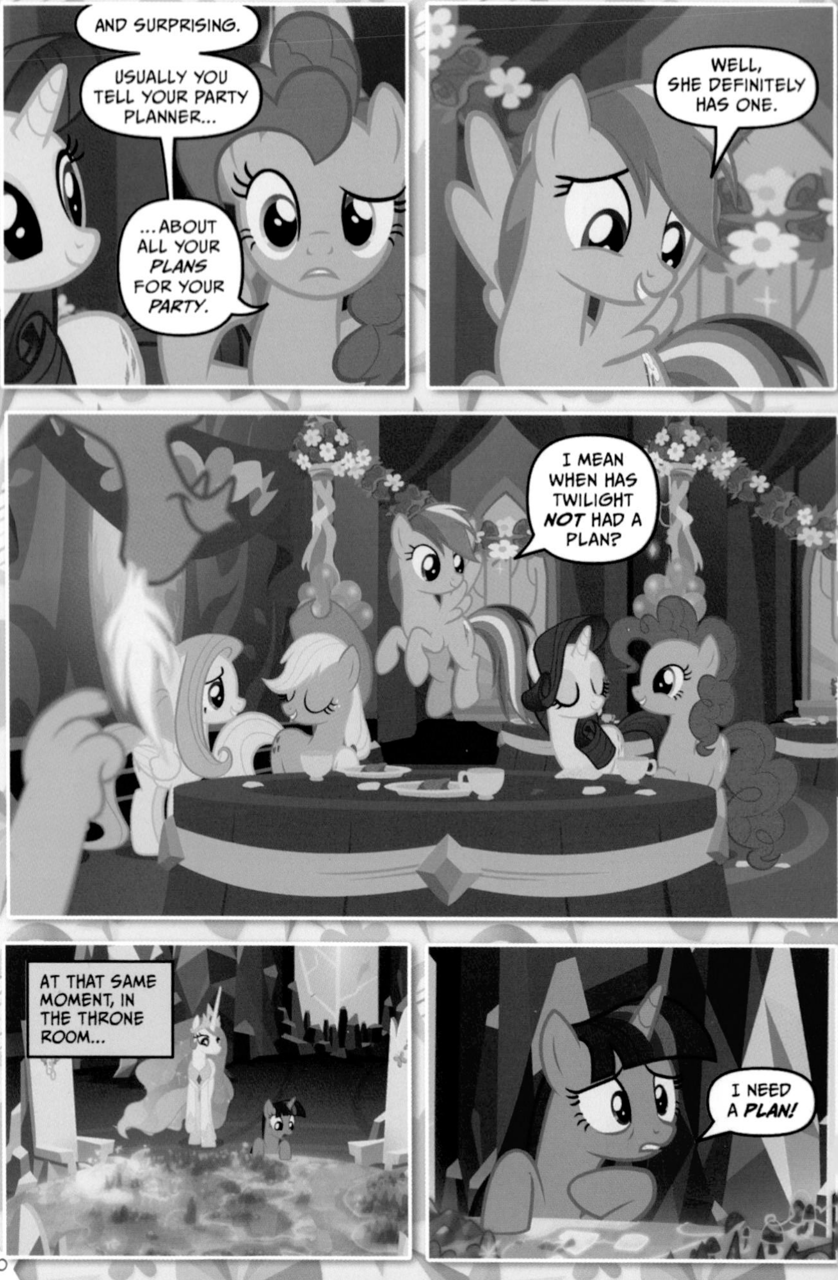
AND SURPRISING.
USUALLY YOU TELL YOUR PARTY PLANNER...
...ABOUT ALL YOUR PLANS FOR YOUR PARTY.
WELL, SHE DEFINITELY HAS ONE.
I MEAN WHEN HAS TWILIGHT NOT HAD A PLAN?
AT THAT SAME MOMENT, IN THE THRONE ROOM...
I NEED A PLAN!

I GOT IT!

SINCE DEFEATING CHRYSALIS...

...STARLIGHT'S GIVEN THE CHANGELINGS AN OPPORTUNITY TO REVOLUTIONIZE THEIR SOCIETY.

MAYBE I CAN SEND HER THERE...

VRROVRRO VRRO

COOL SPELL.

IF STARLIGHT GOES TO THE CHANGELING HIVE...

...SHE CAN HELP THEM ADJUST TO THEIR NEW WAY OF LIFE.

OKAY, FRIENDSHIP ONE-OH-ONE.

THORAX AND I ARE GOING TO SHOW YOU HOW TO COMPROMISE.

I WANT TO HAVE HONEYSUCKLE NECTAR FOR LUNCH.

I WOULD LIKE A SANDWICH.

OH NO.

WHAT SHOULD WE DO?

ATTACK! THE WINNER GETS TO CHOOSE!

OR, THORAX AND I CAN TALK ABOUT IT...

...AND COME UP WITH A SOLUTION THAT WORKS FOR EVERYPONY...

STARLIGHT. HOW DO YOU FEEL ABOUT HONEYSUCKLE AND PEANUT BUTTER SANDWICHES?

WHY, THAT SOUNDS DELICIOUS.

COMPROMISE!

HMMMM...

THIS DOESN'T SEEM LIKE SOMETHING STARLIGHT AND THORAX WOULD DO.

THIS IS TWILIGHT'S FANTASY, SPIKE.

THERE IS NO WRONG WAY TO FANTASIZE.

THANK YOU.

THE CHANGELINGS HAVE SO MUCH TO LEARN ABOUT HOW TO ENJOY LOVE THROUGH FRIENDSHIPS.

STARLIGHT WOULD BE BUSY FOR A VERY LONG TIME...

...BUT HER WORK THERE WOULD BE VERY REWARDING.

OR DANGEROUS!

IT WOULD ONLY TAKE ONE CHANGELING TO DEVIATE FROM THE PACK...

I'LL SHOW STARLIGHT GLIMMER!

SKRRRXXX

SRRRRXXX

HMPF.

HA-HA-HA HA HA.

HI, I'M STARLIGHT GLIMMER. WHAT'S YOUR NAME?

CORNICLE.

HO! HA-HA HA!

WHAT KIND OF NAME IS THAT?

ARE YOU LIKE *BUGS* OR *WHAT?*

SWRRRT

SWACK!!!

FAKE STARLIGHT TROTS OFF...

GET HER!

AS THE REAL ONE RETURNS.

THERE SHE IS!

GET HER!

STOP! WE'LL SHOW HER!

Clop Clop

TWILIGHT'S SEEN ENOUGH!

VRROVRROVRRO

UM, THAT *PROBABLY* WON'T HAPPEN.

BUT IT COULD.

I CAN'T JUST SEND HER OFF TO *CELESTIA-KNOWS-WHERE...*

...WITHOUT THINKING IT THROUGH!

HMMM.

I WAS NOT AWARE THAT I WAS AN EXPRESSION.

AN APPROPRIATE ONE, OF COURSE, FOR EVEN I DON'T KNOW THE ANSWER.

THIS IS A MOMENTOUS DECISION.

YOU MUST CONSIDER *ALL* THE POSSIBILITIES.

RETHINK, RETHINK...

WHAT ABOUT THE DRAGONS?

I CAN SEND STARLIGHT TO THE DRAGON LANDS.

SHE AND EMBER WOULD DEFINITELY HIT IT OFF!

VRRO VRRO VRRO

THE DRAGON LANDS.

VORT

EMBER!

STARLIGHT!

THWAK

YOU READY TO DO SOME DEATH-DEFYING DRAGON STUFF?

TOTALLY.

OKAY, THAT DOESN'T SOUND ANYTHING LIKE EMBER OR STARLIGHT.

WHO KNOWS WHAT THEIR DYNAMIC WOULD BE, SPIKE?

FWOOSH

FWOOSH

VORT

YEAH!

BUMP

STARLIGHT WILL LOVE IT IN THE DRAGON LANDS. IN HER LETTERS, EMBER SAID DRAGONS DO A LOT OF FUN THINGS...

THE FEAST OF FIRES, THE DRAGON BOWL, CLAWCHELLA...

STARLIGHT COULD BE THERE FOR A REALLY LONG TIME.

BUT THEN AGAIN, NOT ALL DRAGONS...

...LIKE PONIES AS MUCH AS EMBER DOES.

HEY, TWINKLE STAR!

IT'S STARLIGHT GLIMMER.

STAR-KLE LIGHT-STAR?

STARLIGHT GLIMMER.

WHATEVER. YOU WANNA HANG WITH US?

BEFORE SHE CAN ANSWER, GARBLE GRABS STARLIGHT...

...AND THEY'RE OFF!

WHAT ARE WE DIVING INTO?

LAVA!

WHAT?!

WOOOOSH

TWILIGHT! THIS IS CRAZY!

VRRPVRRO VRRO

STARLIGHT'S REALLY GOOD WITH MAGIC.

SHE COULD JUST STOP *HERSELF* FROM FALLING INTO A PIT OF LAVA.

WHAT IF SHE DIDN'T REALIZE IT WAS HAPPENING?

YOU JUST NEVER KNOW, SPIKE!!

I JUST NEED TO THINK OF SOMEPLACE SAFE TO SEND HER.

I COULD SEND HER TO THE CRYSTAL EMPIRE...

...TO CONTINUE HER MAGICAL STUDIES WITH SUNBURST!

VRRO VRRO VRRO

IT'LL BE PERFECT!

SUNBURST'S KNOWLEDGE OF MAGIC IS ONLY MATCHED BY STARLIGHT'S ABILITIES.

I GOT IT!

TRY PLACING YOUR HORN DIRECTLY ON THE POTION...

...AND PICTURE THE CLOCK YOU WISH TO MAKE.

VRRRNNN

VIP

IT WORKED!

THEY COULD CHALLENGE EACH OTHER INTO BECOMING THE MOST TALENTED UNICORNS EQUESTRIA HAS EVER SEEN!!

QUICK! WHAT'S NEXT?!

OF COURSE, THE STUDY OF MAGIC IS A LIFELONG PURSUIT...

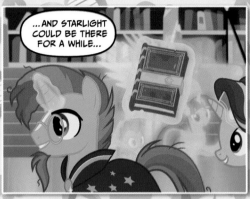

...AND STARLIGHT COULD BE THERE FOR A WHILE...

...ESPECIALLY ONCE THEY START ATTEMPTING THE REALLY *COMPLICATED* STUFF!

SPIKE KNOWS WHERE THIS IS GOING...

THREE, TWO, ONE...

WHAT IF THEY BECOME TOO AMBITIOUS?

I NEVER WOULD HAVE THOUGHT TO COMBINE STARSWIRL'S APPARITION SPELL WITH *SPATIUM FLEXIBUS!*

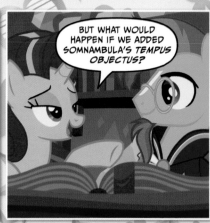

BUT WHAT WOULD HAPPEN IF WE ADDED SOMNAMBULA'S *TEMPUS OBJECTUS?*

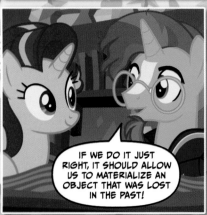

IF WE DO IT JUST RIGHT, IT SHOULD ALLOW US TO MATERIALIZE AN OBJECT THAT WAS LOST IN THE PAST!

OH NO!

SUNBURST USES CHALK TO DRAW THE NECESSARY SYMBOL.

DON'T DO IT!

VRRRNNNN

ZOOOOSH

Gah!

THE PORTAL IS PULLING EVERYTHING INTO ITSELF!

IT'S TOO MUCH!

FWIP

NOOOOOO!

STARLIGHT! NOOOOO!

ZOOOOSH

ZOOOOSH

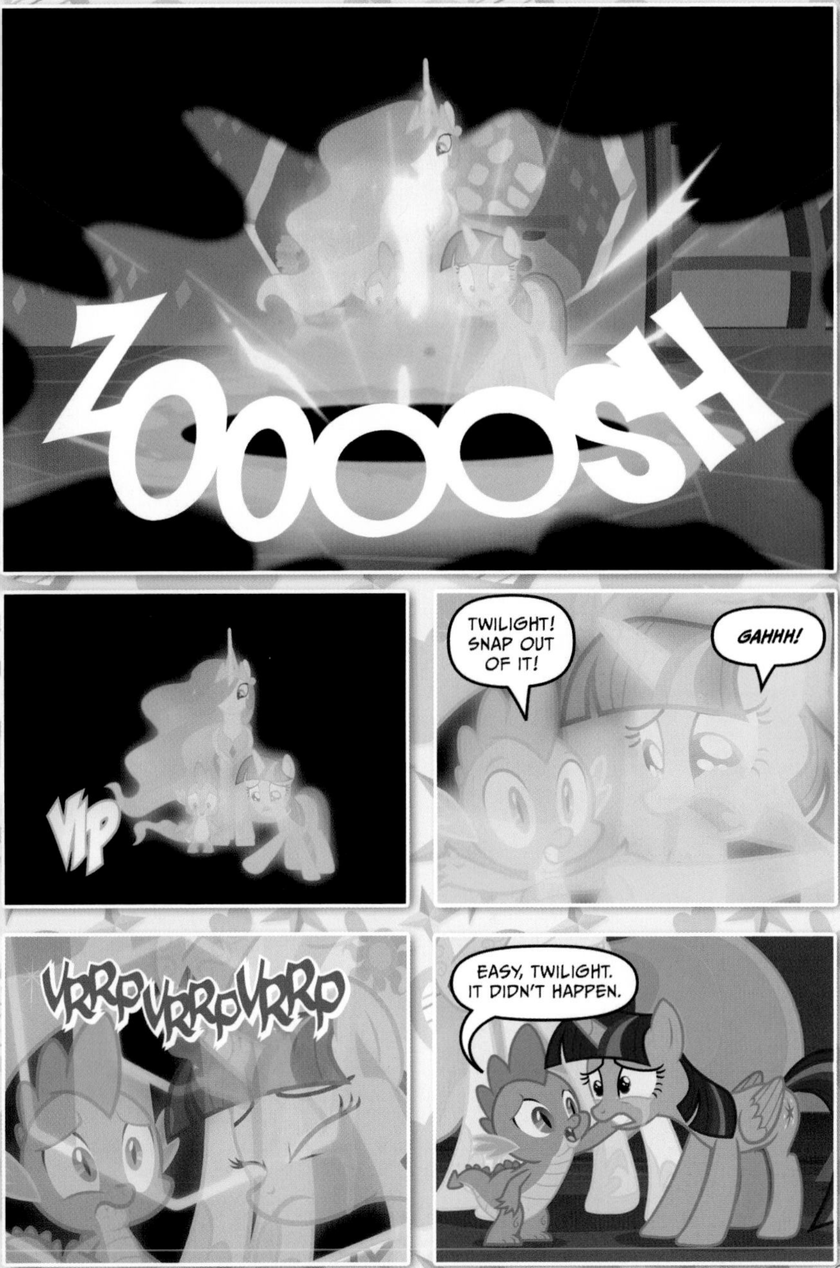
ZOOOOSH
VIP
TWILIGHT! SNAP OUT OF IT!
GAHHH!
VRRP VRRP VRRP
EASY, TWILIGHT. IT DIDN'T HAPPEN.

BUT IT COULD!

I JUST DON'T THINK I CAN SEND HER ANYWHERE.

WHAT AM I GOING TO DO?!

TEE-HEE HEE-HEE!

HA-HA! HO!

HA! HA-HA!

ARE YOU *LAUGHING* AT ME?

I CAN'T BELIEVE YOU'RE LAUGHING AT ME.

OH, TWILIGHT.

I'M NOT.

I'M LAUGHING BECAUSE I HAD THE EXACT SAME FEARS YOU'RE HAVING.

WHAT?!

LET ME TELL YOU A STORY.

ONCE UPON A TIME...

"...THERE WAS A VERY BRIGHT YOUNG FILLY."

"SHE WAS TRULY ONE OF MY BEST STUDENTS."

"ARE YOU TALKING ABOUT TWILIGHT?"

"I CAN'T SEE WHAT YOU'RE THINKING ABOUT!"

"YES, SPIKE."

"I WAS CONSTANTLY *SURPRISED* AND *IMPRESSED* WITH HER DISCOVERIES."

"BUT I NOTICED THAT HER PURSUIT OF ACADEMIA...

"YOU MEAN IT WAS KEEPING HER ISOLATED AND ALONE?"

"UH. YES, SPIKE."

"I HAD A DECISION TO MAKE. BUT IT WASN'T EASY..."

MAYBE I COULD CLOSE THE LIBRARY...

...OR THROW A PARTY IN THE CASTLE?

SHE'D HAVE TO TALK TO THE OTHER FILLIES THEN...

BUT LOOKING AT THE MOON THAT NIGHT, I KNEW THE ANSWER...

I MUST SEND HER AWAY!

"I KNEW THERE WAS A SPECIAL GROUP OF FILLIES IN PONYVILLE...

BACK AT THE CASTLE.

"...BUT I KEPT INVENTING ALL KINDS REASONS WHY I SHOULDN'T SEND YOU..."

WHAT IF SHE RUNS INTO A MANTICORE?

OR WHAT IF SHE GETS PULLED INTO TARTARUS?

OR WORST OF ALL, WHAT IF SHE DOESN'T GET ALONG WITH ANYPONY?

ARE WE SUPPOSED TO SAY SOMETHING?

I DON'T THINK SO.

"I KEPT YOU IN CANTERLOT LONGER THAN I SHOULD HAVE."

EVENTUALLY, I REALIZED ALL THE ANXIETY I FELT...

...WAS BECAUSE *I* DIDN'T WANT YOU TO GO.

REALLY?!

I LOVED HAVING YOU AS A STUDENT.

YOU CHALLENGED ME AND TAUGHT ME...

...JUST AS MUCH AS I TAUGHT YOU.

I AM EMBARRASSED TO ADMIT IT...

...BUT I WAS AFRAID IF YOU MADE FRIENDS...

...YOU WOULDN'T NEED ME ANYMORE.

PRINCESS CELESTIA, THAT IS SO NOT TRUE.

I WILL ALWAYS NEED YOU.

I THINK STARLIGHT GLIMMER MIGHT FEEL THE SAME WAY ABOUT YOU...

...IF THAT'S WHAT YOU'RE AFRAID OF.

MAYBE IT IS. JUST A LITTLE.

OH IT DEFINITELY IS. LIKE A *LOT.*

HERE WE ARE AFTER ALL THESE YEARS, TWILIGHT.

WE'RE LIVING PROOF THAT LETTING SOMEONE SPREAD THEIR WINGS...

...DOESN'T MEAN YOU NO LONGER HAVE A PLACE IN THEIR LIVES.

THANK YOU.

AND IF YOU'RE STILL WORRIED...

...YOU CAN ALWAYS MAKE HER WRITE YOU LETTERS!

WINK

HA HA! I GET IT!

BACK AT THE RECEPTION...

...TWILIGHT RETURNS WITH A GIFT.

VRRRNNN

AND A HUSH FALLS OVER THE CROWD.

A SPOTLIGHT TURNS ON AND BLINDS TWILIGHT.

GLUNK

I MAY HAVE LET IT SLIP THAT YOU'D BE UNVEILING YOUR BIG PLAN FOR STARLIGHT TONIGHT.

SILLY ME. BUT WE'RE ALL VERY EXCITED TO HEAR WHAT YOU'VE COOKED UP.

TWILIGHT LOOKS OUT INTO THE CROWD...

...AND...

OH NO!

YOU WEREN'T COMING UP WITH A PLAN JUST NOW...

...WERE YOU?

OH DEAR. THIS COULD BE PRETTY EMBARRASSING FOR YOU.

GEE, THANKS DISCORD.

ANYTIME. I REALLY DO LOVE BEING HELPFUL.

POOF

KUNK

KUNK

AS YOU ALL KNOW, STARLIGHT GLIMMER HAS BEEN MY PUPIL FOR A WHILE NOW...

...AND I HOPED SHE'D BE MY PUPIL FOR A LONG TIME YET TO COME...

...BUT IT TURNS OUT THAT'S *JUST NOT MEANT TO BE.*

Gah—!

STARLIGHT, YOU HAVE PROVED YOURSELF TO BE A KIND, LOYAL, STRONG, HONEST AND TRULY MAGICAL FRIEND.

I JUST HAVE TO LOOK AROUND THIS ROOM AT ALL THE NEW FRIENDSHIPS YOU'VE MADE...

...TO KNOW THAT THERE IS NOTHING MORE I NEED TO TEACH YOU.

SO WE HAVE A SECOND REASON TO CELEBRATE TODAY.

THREE CHEERS FOR STARLIGHT GLIMMER ON HER "GRADUATION" DAY!

HOORAY! HOORAY! HOORAY!

EEEEEEE—!

WHAT A *GREAT* SURPRISE!

YOUR FUTURE IS IN YOUR OWN HOOVES NOW.

REALLY? WOW.

I WAS NOT EXPECTING THIS.

SQUEEEEZE

DARN IT. I WAS HOPING YOU WOULD SEND HER TO MY REALM.

WE COULD HAVE BEEN ROOMIES!

WAY TO NOT PICK UP WHAT I WAS PUTTING DOWN.

HOW DO YOU WANNA CELEBRATE?

GIRLS TRIP TO LAS PEGASUS?

WE CAN THROW YOU A CHANGELING GORBFEST!

IT'S MORE FUN THAN IT SOUNDS.

OR WE COULD GO CAUSE A LITTLE MISCHIEF.

I KNOW A TRICK THAT'LL TURN CELESTIA'S CASTLE INTO CHEESE.

DO YOU THINK IT'S A *GOUDA* IDEA? HA!

THAT'S JUST THE FIRST OF MANY CHEESE JOKES IF WE GO DOWN THIS PATH.

THAT ALL SOUNDS WONDERFUL BUT UM...

GIVE ME A MINUTE, WOULD YA?

STARLIGHT GOES TO JOIN TWILIGHT...

CONGRATULATIONS!

THANKS!

SO, HOW DO YOU FEEL?

HAPPY, SURPRISED, OVER-WHELMED...

I MEAN, NOT THAT I'M NOT GRATEFUL, BUT ARE YOU SURE?

BELIEVE ME, I'VE THOUGHT LONG AND HARD ABOUT THIS.

OF COURSE YOU DID.

STARLIGHT, TRUST ME. YOU'RE READY.

NO, I'M NOT.

I'M NOT READY TO LEAVE!

OH GOOD! CUZ I'M NOT READY FOR THAT EITHER!

HERE. I GOT YOU THIS PRESENT.

VRRRNNN

SHE OPENS THE BOX AND...

IT WAS GOING TO BE A "CONGRATS ON GETTING A MEDAL OF HONOR PRESENT"...

...BUT THEN I WAS AFRAID IT WOULD HAVE TO BE A "GOING AWAY" PRESENT...

...BUT NOW IT'S A "I COULDN'T BE HAPPIER YOU'RE STAYING" PRESENT!

IT FITS PERFECTLY OVER YOUR DRESSER.

I KNOW. I MEASURED!

THANK YOU.

I MAY NOT KNOW WHAT COMES NEXT FOR YOU, BUT WHATEVER IT IS...

...I PROMISE I'LL ALWAYS BE THERE FOR YOU.

SQUEEEEEEZE

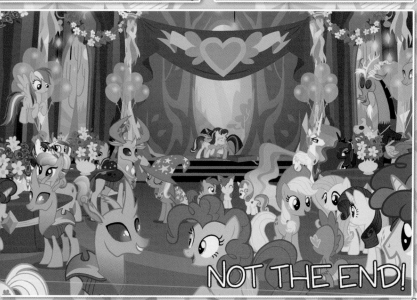

NOT THE END!

ALL BOTTLED UP

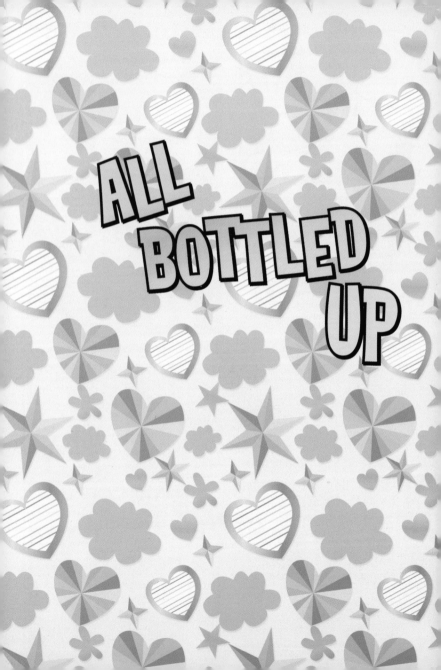

ANOTHER FINE DAY IN *PONYVILLE*.

AND TRIXIE IS WORKING ON HER MAGIC.

ZRRRNNN

COME ON...

...TURN INTO A TEA CUP!

VRRRNNNG

NO! TEA CUP!

STARLIGHT, I CAN'T PUT A TRICK THAT'S NOT WORKING INTO MY ACT.

HOW COME IT'S NOT WORKING?

IT COULD BE BECAUSE YOU'RE JUST YELLING "TEA CUP..."

...AND NOT PICTURING IT IN YOUR MIND.

OH. YEAH, THAT COULD BE IT.

WHAT DOES YOUR TEA CUP LOOK LIKE?

WHAT SHAPE IS IT?

WHAT COLOR?

VRRRNNNG

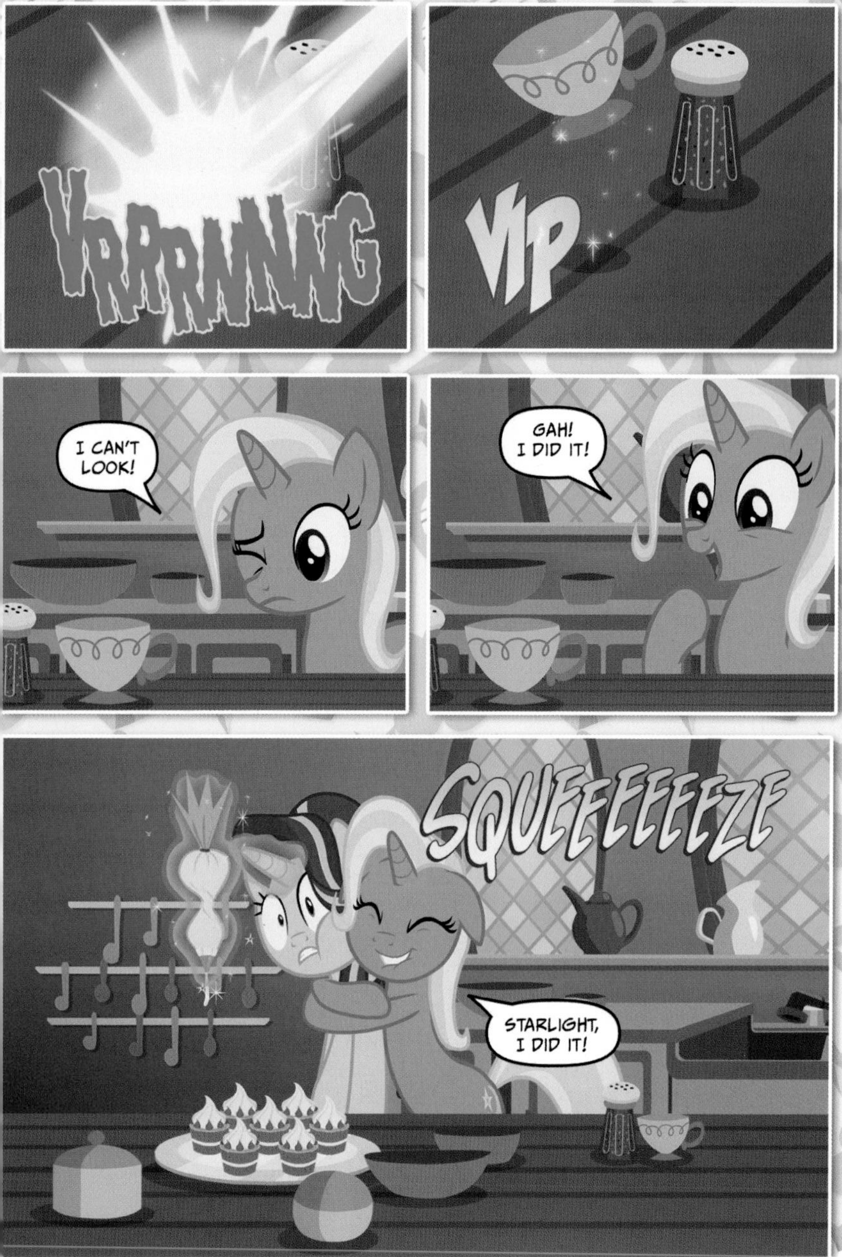
VRRRRNNNG
VIP
I CAN'T LOOK!
GAH! I DID IT!
SQUEEEEEEEZE
STARLIGHT, I DID IT!

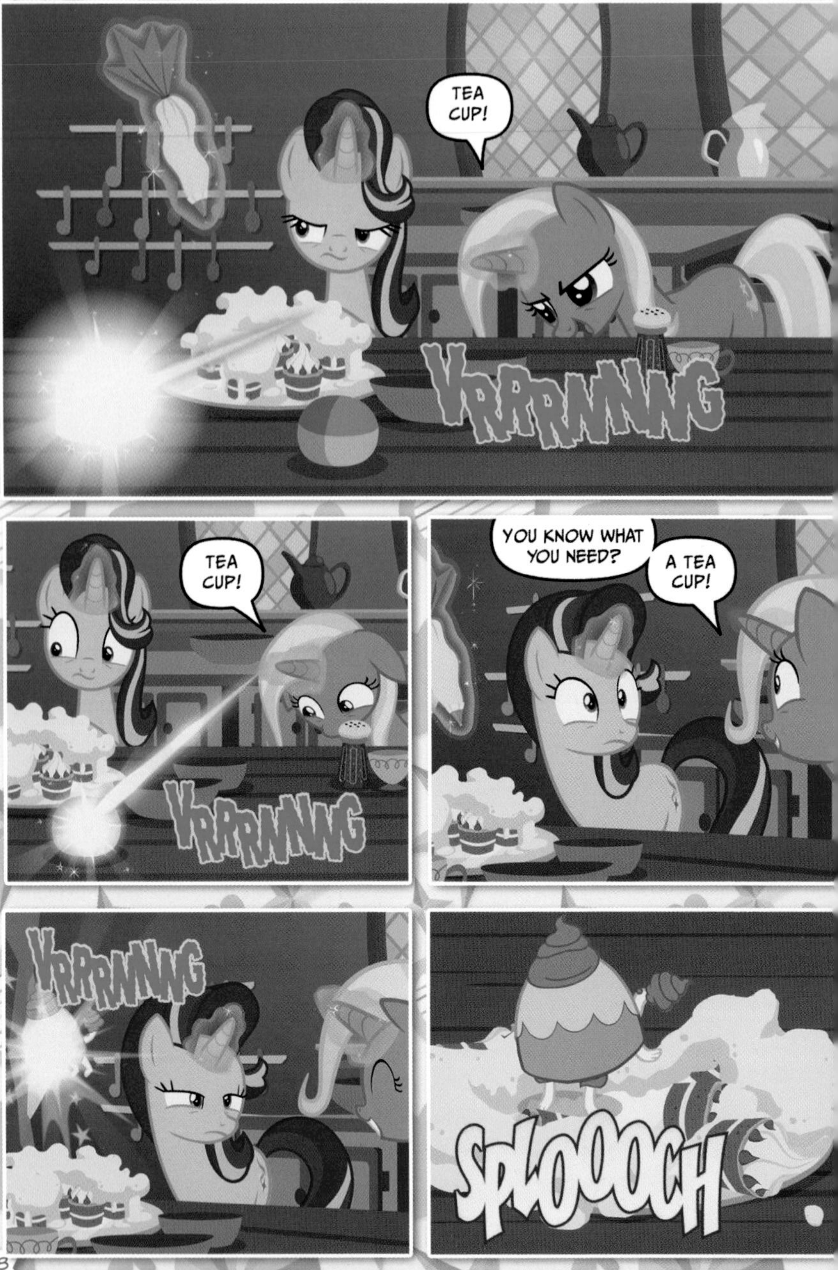
TEA CUP!
VRRRRWNNG
TEA CUP!
VRRRRWNNG
YOU KNOW WHAT YOU NEED?
A TEA CUP!
VRRRRWNNG
SPLOOOCH

WHOOPS!

DOINK

I GUESS I PICTURED A TEA CUP POODLE.

TRIXIE, YOU RUINED MY TEA CAKES!

THEY WERE ALMOST DONE!

I JUST GOT EXCITED!

THIS IS THE FIRST TIME I DID A *TRANSFIGURATION* SPELL.

REAL MAGIC!

C'MON. BE IMPRESSED BY ME!

"YAY TRIXIE! YOU ARE SO GREAT AT MAGIC AND HAVING GOOD HAIR."

GOOD JOB, TRIX...

...BUT I WAS BAKING THESE TO GIVE TO TWILIGHT AND THE GIRLS...

...FOR THEIR FRIENDSHIP RETREAT.

PINKIE PIE GAVE ME HER RECIPE AND EVERYTHING.

YOU NEED SNACKS FOR TWILIGHT AND THE GIRLS?

I HAVE JUST WHAT YOU WANT.

STARLIGHT IS NOT SO SURE...

90

SPLAT

PROBLEM SOLVED?

HSSSSSS

NOT EXACTLY.

CHOOOOOO

I AM SO EXCITED FOR THIS FRIENDSHIP RETREAT!

I CAN'T REMEMBER THE LAST TIME WE ALL GOT TO HANG OUT...

...WITHOUT HAVING TO SAVE EQUESTRIA!

WE ARE AWESOME...

...BUT TECHNICALLY WE WEREN'T THE LAST PONIES TO SAVE EQUESTRIA...

I WAS SPEAKING IN A BROADER SENSE!

ARE YOU SURE YOU TWO DON'T WANT TO COME WITH US?

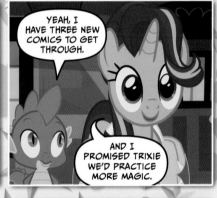

YEAH, I HAVE THREE NEW COMICS TO GET THROUGH.

AND I PROMISED TRIXIE WE'D PRACTICE MORE MAGIC.

IT MIGHT BE BETTER IF THE CASTLE WAS EMPTY...

...IF YOU KNOW WHAT I MEAN.

UGH. RELAX.

IF ANYTHING BREAKS...

...STARLIGHT WILL JUST GO BACK IN TIME AND FIX IT.

THE LOOK ON HER FACE SAYS "MAYBE WE'VE DONE THAT BEFORE!"

HA HA, DON'T BE SILLY.

KIDDING!

WE'LL TAKE GOOD CARE OF THE CASTLE WHILE YOU'RE GONE.

HAVE FUN ON YOUR FRIENDSHIP RETREAT!

WHAT IN EQUESTRIA IS A FRIENDSHIP RETREAT, ANYWAY?

THEY'RE GONNA BOND, SHARE LAUGHS...

...AND IF I KNOW THEM...

...THEY'RE GONNA SING A SONG.

HEE-HEE! WE'RE GONNA HAVE SO MUCH MORE FUN THAN THEM.

SHHHHH!

TWILIGHT, WAIT!

STARLIGHT HAS SOMETHING FOR YOU!

HUH?!

THANKS A LOT, TRIXIE!

HERE, I, UM, BROUGHT YOU SNACKS.

OH. HOW... *THOUGHTFUL.* THANKS.

WE WILL... NOT GET HUNGRY ON THE TRAIN.

CATCHING TWILIGHT'S DISAPPOINTMENT...

IT WAS SUPPOSED TO BE TEA CAKES...

...BUT IT'S A *LONG* STORY.

NOT THAT IT MATTERS.

HAVE A GREAT TIME!

WE WILL! YOU TOO!

CHOOO CHOOOO

EQUESTRIA'S NEWEST HEROES WATCH THEIR FRIENDS HEAD INTO THE DISTANCE...

WE'RE GONNA HAVE SO MUCH FUN.

BACK AT THE CASTLE.

OKAY TRIXIE...

...WHAT KIND OF SPELLS DID YOU WANT TO WORK ON NEXT?

WELL, EVERY SELF-RESPECTING MAGICIAN HAS A DISAPPEARING ACT...

...SO MAYBE WE CAN START WITH THAT?

HMM. NOTHING JUST DISAPPEARS...

...SO THAT'S TECHNICALLY A TELEPORTATION SPELL...

...AND THOSE ARE PRETTY HARD.

MAYBE WE SHOULD START WITH SOMETHING SMALLER?

NO, NO, NO!

THE **GREAT** AND **POWERFUL** TRIXIE GOES BIG... OR NOT AT ALL!

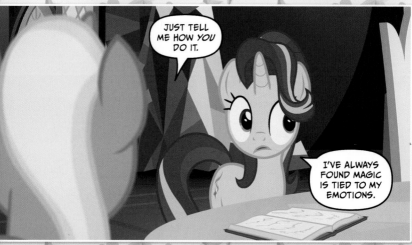

JUST TELL ME HOW *YOU* DO IT.

I'VE ALWAYS FOUND MAGIC IS TIED TO MY EMOTIONS.

WHATEVER I'M FEELING FUELS WHATEVER I'M DOING...

...AND THE STRONGER I'M FEELING THE STRONGER THE MAGIC.

RIGHT.

LIKE WHEN YOU WERE SO UPSET THAT CUTIE MARKS TOOK AWAY YOUR FRIEND...

...YOUR MAGIC WAS STRONG ENOUGH TO ENSLAVE AN ENTIRE VILLAGE.

HISSSSS

YUP. THANKS FOR BRINGING THAT UP.

SEE? I'M ALREADY LEARNING!

IF *ANYPONY* IS GOING TO TEACH ME HOW TO DO A *DISAPPEARING* SPELL...

TELEPORTATION SPELL.

WHATEVER.

I'M COMPLIMENTING YOU!

AND ME.

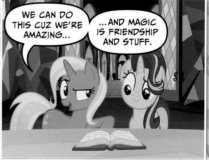

WE CAN DO THIS CUZ WE'RE AMAZING...

...AND MAGIC IS FRIENDSHIP AND STUFF.

HA-HA, OKAY.

I GUESS WE CAN GIVE IT A WHIRL.

NOW, WE JUST NEED TO FIND YOU *SOMETHING* TO *TELEPORT.*

SPIKE!

HOW ABOUT IT?

SPIKE'S A *GOOD SPORT...*

UH— HA HA?

...BUT HE KNOWS A *BAD IDEA* WHEN HE HEARS IT.

FWIP

LET'S PICK SOMETHING, I DON'T KNOW, NOT LIVING.

I MEAN, IT WON'T BE AS IMPRESSIVE, BUT OKAY.

TEACH AWAY, MINI TWILIGHT!

GRRRR.

MEANWHILE, IN *MANEHATTAN*.

WELCOME TO MANEHATTAN ESCAPES!

I'M GOING TO START WITH A FACIAL, THEN GET MY HOOVES DONE...

OH. IT'S NOT THAT KIND OF RETREAT.

ISN'T IT CALLED *MANEHATTAN ESCAPES*...

...BECAUSE IT'S A *DELUXE SPA*...

...WHERE YOU CAN *ESCAPE* ALL YOUR TROUBLES?

NOPE.

IT'S BECAUSE WE GET LOCKED IN A ROOM...

...AND WE HAVE TO SOLVE *PUZZLES* AND *RIDDLES* IN ORDER TO ESCAPE!

CREEEEK

WELCOME TO YOUR ROOM.

THE CLUES WILL LEAD YOU TO A KEY TO GET OUT.

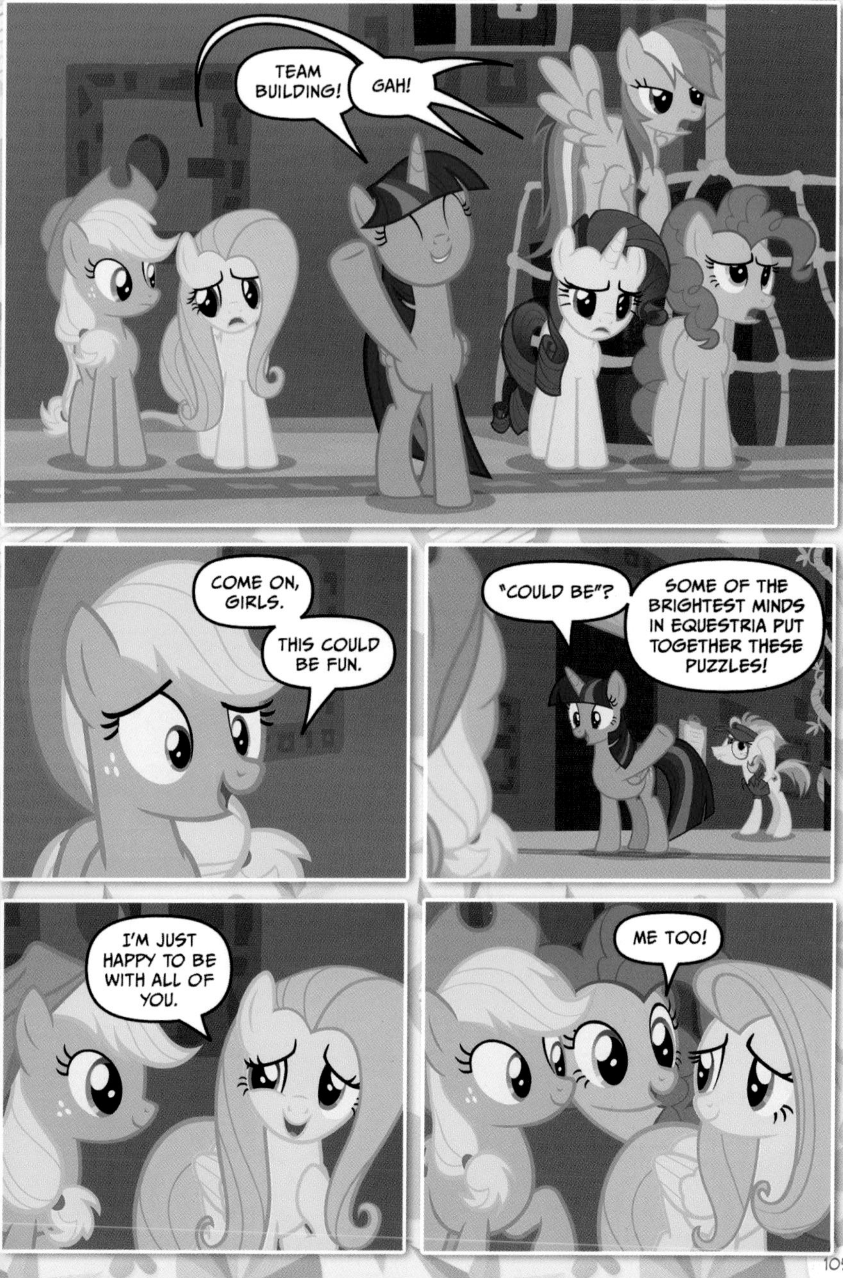
TEAM BUILDING!
GAH!
COME ON, GIRLS.
THIS COULD BE FUN.
"COULD BE"?
SOME OF THE BRIGHTEST MINDS IN EQUESTRIA PUT TOGETHER THESE PUZZLES!
I'M JUST HAPPY TO BE WITH ALL OF YOU.
ME TOO!

I'M NOT GREAT AT SOLVING RIDDLES...

...BUT I'M SUPER GREAT AT CHEERING OTHER PONIES ON WHILE THEY DO IT.

GO US!

YES, YES, BUT JUST SO WE KNOW, *EXACTLY*...

...HOW LONG *WILL* WE BE LOCKED IN HERE?

IT SAYS HERE THAT A GROUP OF GRIFFONS SET THE RECORD FOR THE FASTEST ESCAPE.

IT ONLY TOOK THEM AN HOUR.

PSSH. GRIFFONS BARELY LIKE EACH OTHER...

...AND WE'RE BASICALLY THE POSTER PONIES FOR AMAZING FRIENDSHIPS.

SO GET YOUR QUILL READY, BUB.

YOU'RE GONNA HAVE TO WRITE DOWN A NEW RECORD.

BUMP

BACK IN PONYVILLE...

IF YOU MASTER THIS SPELL BEFORE THE GIRLS GET BACK...

ZRRRNNNNN

YOU'D BE SETTING SOME KIND OF RECORD.

CHALLENGE ACCEPTED.

OKAY, WHAT YOU WANT TO DO IS...

...*CONCENTRATE* ON THE OBJECT THAT YOU WANT TO TELEPORT.

YEAH, I'M GONNA GO—

FWOOSH

—ALL THE WAY...

...OVER HERE.

CONCENTRATE ON TELEPORTING, GOT IT.

Doin' the spell!

TRIX, WAIT. NOT JUST—

VRRRNNNN

VIP

AND THE MAP IS GONE!

TOK

GWAH~!

WHUMP

TA-DA!

MOMENTS LATER...

NONONONO NONONO!

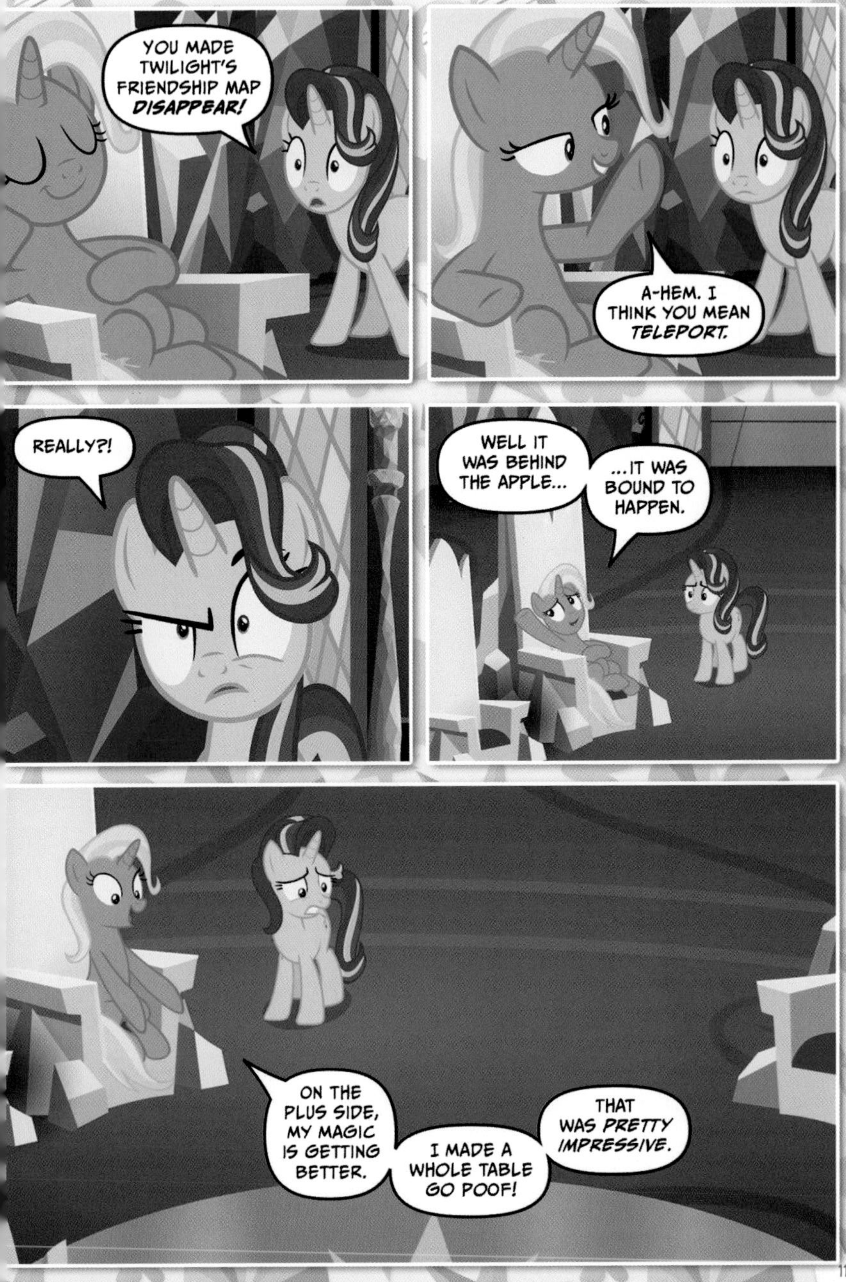
YOU MADE TWILIGHT'S FRIENDSHIP MAP DISAPPEAR!
A-HEM. I THINK YOU MEAN TELEPORT.
REALLY?!
WELL IT WAS BEHIND THE APPLE...
...IT WAS BOUND TO HAPPEN.
ON THE PLUS SIDE, MY MAGIC IS GETTING BETTER.
I MADE A WHOLE TABLE GO POOF!
THAT WAS PRETTY IMPRESSIVE.

TRIXIE, WE HAVE TO GET THAT MAP BACK.

TWILIGHT'S NEVER GOING TO TRUST ME TO BE ALONE IN THIS CASTLE AGAIN!

WHAT WERE YOU *THINKING?*

"TELEPORT"! LIKE YOU TOLD ME TO!

PSSSSSSH

NO! YOU'RE SUPPOSED TO CONCENTRATE ON THE OBJECT!

NOT JUST TELEPORTING!

GEEZ, YOU PROBABLY SHOULD HAVE TOLD ME ALL THE STEPS...

...BEFORE YOU LET ME DO THE SPELL.

I TRIED!

GAH!

I... I...

AND THAT'S WHEN STARLIGHT NOTICED THE CLOUD SPEWING FROM HER HORN.

I NEED A MINUTE.

MEANWHILE, SPIKE'S BEEN WASHING *A LOT* OF TEA CUPS.

BWHUMP

HEY, ARE YOU OKAY?

I WILL BE...

...ONCE I CAST A SPELL TO CONTAIN MY ANGER IN THIS BOTTLE.

WAIT... WHAT?!

DID YOU SEE THAT STORM CLOUD?

THIS HAS NEVER HAPPENED BEFORE!

ALL THAT ANGRY MAGICAL ENERGY HAS TO GO SOMEWHERE...

...AND IF I'M NOT USING IT TO FIGHT A MAGICAL DUEL...

...OR BEND MY FRIENDS' WILLS TO OBEY MY EVERY COMMAND—

HA! I REMEMBER THAT.

THE POINT IS, I DON'T KNOW WHAT MY MAGIC'S GOING TO DO.

SO I'M HOPING IF I BOTTLE UP MY ANGER...

...I WON'T DO WHO-KNOWS-WHAT TO TRIXIE.

ARE YOU SURE THAT'S A GOOD IDEA?

WHAT CHOICE DO I HAVE?

I HAVE TO GET THAT MAP BACK AND I DON'T WANT TO LOSE TRIXIE.

IF SHE KNEW WHAT I WAS THINKING RIGHT NOW...

...SHE'D PROBABLY NEVER TALK TO ME AGAIN.

OKAY. YOU DO WHAT YOU NEED TO DO.

I'LL SEE IF I CAN FIND THE MAP SOMEWHERE IN THE CASTLE.

SQUIP

ZRRRNWN

POP

ZRRRNXN

WITH HER ANGER BOTTLED...

...STARLIGHT PUTS THE BOTTLE SOMEWHERE SAFE.

THAT'S BETTER.

WHERE SHE CAN KEEP IT CLOSE BY.

THEN HEADS BACK TO JOIN TRIXIE.

Clop Clop

TRIXIE...

OH! THERE YOU ARE!

FOR A MINUTE THERE I DIDN'T THINK YOU WERE COMING BACK...

...AND THAT YOU MIGHT BE UPSET WITH ME FOR SOME WEIRD REASON.

BUT THEN I REMEMBERED YOU NEVER GET MAD AT ME.

PSSSSH

ZRRRNNN

PLOP

NOPE. NOT MAD AT ALL.

SO, THE MAP IS PROBABLY IN THE LAST PLACE YOU WERE THINKING OF.

WHERE WAS THAT?

OOOH. GREAT QUESTION.

I WISH YOU HAD ASKED IT LIKE RIGHT AFTER I DID THE SPELL.

I DON'T REMEMBER ANYMORE.

PSSSSSH

STARLIGHT FIGHTS TO CONTAIN HER ANGER!

ZRRRNNN

NO WORRIES. WE'LL JUST TAKE A WALK AROUND TOWN.

MAYBE THAT WILL JOG YOUR MEMORY.

OK, THAT SOUNDS FUN.

OOOH!

DID YOU REMEMBER?

NO. BUT I THINK WE SHOULD STOP FOR CINNAMON NUTS WHILE WE'RE OUT!

CINNAMON.

NUTS!

THAT'S A GOOD IDEA.

YESSSSS! I'VE BEEN CRAVING SOMETHING SWEET...

...SINCE I COULDN'T HAVE ANY TEA CAKES THIS MORNING.

IT'S GONNA BE A LONG DAY.

YOU GOT THIS, STARLIGHT.

BACK IN *MANEHATTAN*...

YOU GOT THIS, TWILIGHT!

YOU CAN DO IT!

HOO-WEE!

YOU SOLVED THAT TRIANGLE-Y THING MIGHTY FAST.

DOES ANYPONY NEED A PURPLE JEWEL?

OOH! PLUM OR BOYSENBERRY?

DON'T BOTH THOSE FRUITS MEAN "PURPLE"?

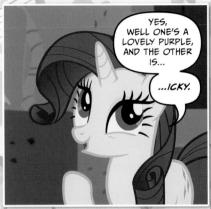

YES, WELL ONE'S A LOVELY PURPLE, AND THE OTHER IS...

...ICKY.

JUST PUT THE GEM IN!

WE'RE TRYING TO SET A RECORD, HERE!

FLUTTERSHY TAKES RAINBOW DASH'S ADVICE!

CLICK

THERE!

FRRRRP

THE TAPESTRY RETRACTS...

...TO REVEAL A SCROLL!

LOOK AT THAT!

BACK IN PONYVILLE...

...TIME IS *EATING* AT STARLIGHT.

CRUNCH CRUNCH

HELLO, PONIES, HOW CAN I HELP YOU?

OOH, ARE THOSE CINNAMON NUTS?

YES! I GOT THEM FROM THE CART OUTSIDE.

123

DO YOU WANT SOME?

STARLIGHT DECIDES THERE'S NO TIME FOR THAT.

FWIP

ZRRRNNN

HAVE YOU SEEN A BIG TABLE?

MAGICAL MAP ON IT?

SOMETIMES GLOWING CUTIE MARKS SHOOT OUT?

NO. WHY IN EQUESTRIA WOULD SOMETHING LIKE THAT BE HERE?

I CAST A PRETTY AMAZING SPELL THAT TRANSPORTED IT TO THE LAST PLACE I WAS THINKING OF.

BUT I MIGHT HAVE BEEN THINKING ABOUT...

...HOW I'D TREAT MYSELF TO A NICE BROOCH IF I PULLED IT OFF.

AH. WELL, NO HUGE TABLE HERE.

BUT ARE YOU STILL INTERESTED IN THAT BROOCH?

SURE

NO!

HEADING OUT OF THE STORE...

PsssssSH

WE DON'T HAVE TIME FOR THIS!!

TWILIGHT AND THE GIRLS ARE GONNA BE BACK SOON.

BUT I'M NOT UPSET.

WHAT'S OUR NEXT STOP?

SWEET APPLE ACRES.

NOPE.

HAVEN'T SEEN IT.

ARE YOU SURE?

IT'S REALLY, REALLY IMPORTANT THAT WE FIND IT.

AND IT MIGHT BE HERE BECAUSE—

—SOMEPONY WAS CRAVING APPLES.

I'M STILL CRAVING THEM.

THEY'D GO WELL WITH CINNAMON NUTS!

THOSE NUTS SURE DO SMELL GOOD!

GRANNY SMITH. *PLEASE.*

THE TABLE?

MY EYES AIN'T WHAT THEY USED TO BE...

...BUT I'D KNOW *FER* SURE IF A HUGE TABLE APPEARED OUT OF THIN AIR!

≩SIGH≩ WELL, WE TRIED.

MOMENTS LATER...

I COULD'VE SWORN IT'D BE AT THE ICE CREAM PARLOR...

...BECAUSE IT WAS WARM IN THE CASTLE...

...AND I THOUGHT I WANTED ICE CREAM.

MAYBE WE SHOULD CHECK OUT THE CRYSTAL EMPIRE...

127

PsSSSSH

BECAUSE TWILIGHT'S CASTLE IS MADE OUT OF CRYSTALS...

...SO I TOTALLY HAD CRYSTALS ON MY MIND.

STARLIGHT DOESN'T EVEN RESPOND.

SHE JUST BOTTLES HER REACTION...

...BUT IT'S TAKING A TOLL!

OKAY.

WE BETTER START MOVING IF WE WANT TO MAKE IT TO THE CRYSTAL EMPIRE.

ARE YOU OKAY, STARLIGHT?

BECAUSE YOU SEEM A LITTLE...WHAT'S THE WORD?

DRAB.

PsSSSSH

ZRRRNNN

BUT THIS TIME TRIXIE NOTICES!

I AM GREAT.

DID YOUR SADDLE BAG JUST GLOW?

NO.

WHAT'S IN THERE?!

YOU SHOW ME WHAT IS IN THAT BAG!

CINNAMON NUTS!

VRRRNNN

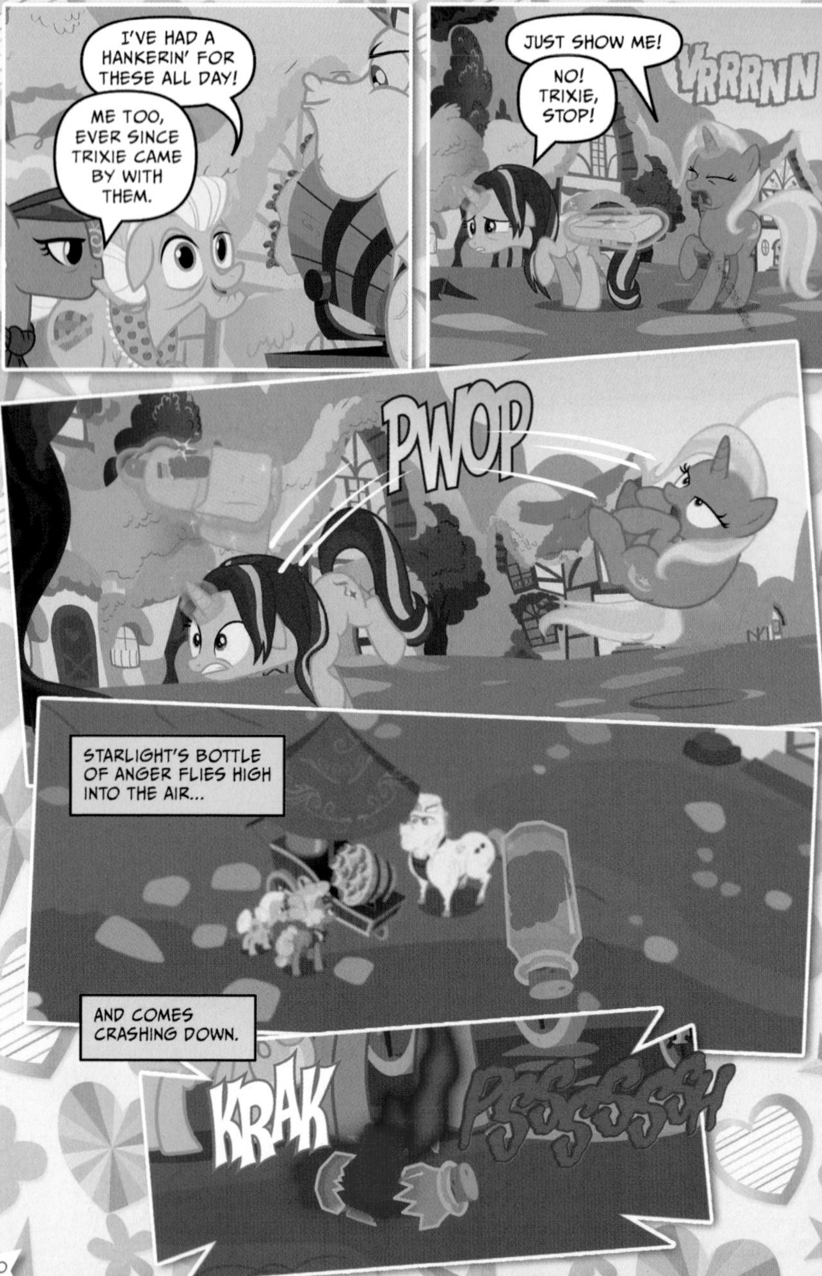
I'VE HAD A HANKERIN' FOR THESE ALL DAY!
ME TOO, EVER SINCE TRIXIE CAME BY WITH THEM.
JUST SHOW ME!
NO! TRIXIE, STOP!
VRRRNN
PWOP
STARLIGHT'S BOTTLE OF ANGER FLIES HIGH INTO THE AIR...
AND COMES CRASHING DOWN.
KRAK
PSSSSSH

GAH!

AS STARLIGHT'S ANGER ESCAPES...

...IT FINDS NEW PONIES TO UPSET!

WHY ARE THEY LOOKING AT ME LIKE THAT?

YOU RUINED MY TEA CAKES!

WHAT?!

YOU JUST HAD TO GIVE TWILIGHT THOSE *SMELLY* PRETZELS.

WERE THEY YOUR PRETZELS?

I DON'T UNDERSTAND—

YOU *DON'T* PAY ATTENTION WHEN I'M TRYING TO TEACH YOU!

STARLIGHT, CAN YOU HELP ME... PLEASE!

IN THE ESCAPE ROOM...

UM, TWILIGHT...

VRRRNNN

...CAN YOU HELP ME, PLEASE?

TWILIGHT REMOVES THE BLOCKS WITH HER MAGIC...

I'VE SEEN THOSE SYMBOLS...

...OVER HERE!

TWO OTHER PONIES TOUCH THEIR PANELS...

VUT

VUT

YOU CAN DO IT!

...AND THE TRAP DOOR FALLS OPEN!

ALMOST THERE!

flip

OH MY GOSH, I'VE GOT THE KEY!

chomp

QUICK, GET IT IN THE LOCK!

THIS IS IT!

I'M SO IMPRESSED.

I'M NOT. I ALREADY KNEW WE WERE THE *BEST.*

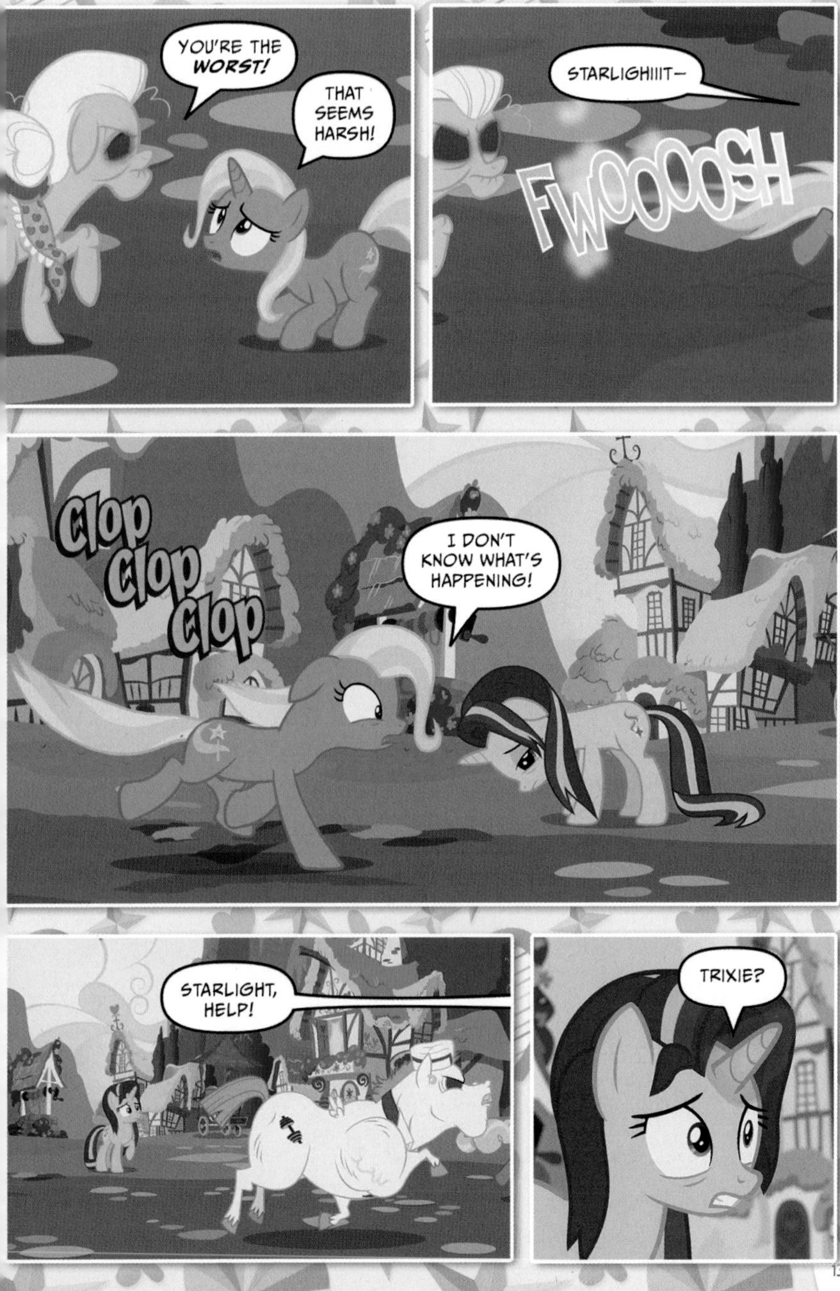
YOU'RE THE WORST!
THAT SEEMS HARSH!
STARLIGHIIIT—
FWOOOOSH
Clop Clop Clop
I DON'T KNOW WHAT'S HAPPENING!
STARLIGHT, HELP!
TRIXIE?

STARLIGHT GOES TO READY A BLAST...

...BUT SHE DOESN'T HAVE THE ENERGY.

Puff.

I'M GLAD TWILIGHT ISN'T HERE TO SEE THIS.

I REALLY WISH STARLIGHT WERE HERE TO SEE HOW STRONG FRIENDSHIPS CAN BE...

...WHEN WE TRUST EACH OTHER AND WORK TOGETHER.

YOU'VE ALL TAUGHT ME SO MUCH.

THAT WAS A GREAT SPEECH.

BUT, UM, YOU KNOW...

...THE GAME ISN'T OVER UNTIL YOU TURN THAT KEY.

GAH!

chomp

click

DID WE DO IT?

tick

SO CLOSE.

YOU MISSED THE GRIFFON RECORD BY TWO SECONDS.

WITHOUT THAT SPEECH YOU'D PROBABLY HAVE BEATEN IT.

AH NUTS!

AWW NUTS!

YOU JUST DO WHATEVER YOU WANT TO DO!

TRIXIE MAKES A BREAK FOR IT!

Clop Clop

STARLIGHT!

SKREEEEEE

AND YOU DON'T ALWAYS HAVE TO BRING UP MY DARK PAST!

I DIDN'T KNOW YOU HAD ONE, GRANNY SMITH!

WELL!

Thump

FWIP FWIP FWIP

GAH!

139

I JUST CAN'T BELIEVE YOU SOMETIMES!

YOU MAKE ME SO *MAD!*

I BARELY EVEN KNOW YOU!

I DON'T UNDERSTAND WHY YOU'RE ALL MAD AT ME!

THEY'RE NOT.

I AM.

YOU ARE?

I'M REALLY... MAD AT YOU.

YOU LOST TWILIGHT'S MAP TABLE!

YOU MAKE JOKES LIKE IT'S NO BIG DEAL!

IT'S LIKE YOU DON'T EVEN CARE YOU COULD GET ME IN A LOT OF TROUBLE.

IF WE CAN'T FIND THAT TABLE...

...TWILIGHT'S NEVER GOING TO TRUST ME AGAIN.

AND THE WORST PART IS...

YOU NEVER EVEN SAID YOU WERE SORRY!

I'M...

I'M SORRY.

I HAD NO IDEA YOU FELT THAT WAY.

KRAKADOOM

YEAH! I DO!

STARLIGHT STOPS HERSELF AND TAKES A DEEP BREATH.

B-SHFEFF

AND HER CLOUD DISAPPEARS.

BUT TO BE FAIR, I DON'T KNOW HOW YOU COULD HAVE KNOWN.

I DID A SPELL SO YOU WOULDN'T BE ABLE TO TELL. I BOTTLED UP MY ANGER...

...BUT THE BOTTLE BROKE, AND INFECTED THESE THREE.

I AM REALLY SORRY.

I USED MAGIC SO I WOULDN'T USE MAGIC.

I SHOULD HAVE GUESSED THAT WOULD BACKFIRE.

THAT'S ALRIGHT. IT WAS A SLOW DAY.

YEAH. I WAS JUST GONNA GET MY DENTURES CLEANED BEFORE Y'ALL SHOWED UP.

OH NO! MY NUT CART!

VRRRNNN

YAY! MY NUT CART!

AS THE VILLAGERS HEAD THEIR SEPARATE DIRECTIONS...

NOT GONNA LIE...

...HEARING YOU AND THOSE RANDOM PONIES...

...SAY ALL THOSE TERRIBLE THINGS ABOUT ME WASN'T EASY.

BUT I NEEDED TO HEAR IT.

WHY DIDN'T YOU JUST TELL ME HOW YOU FELT?

I DIDN'T WANT TO LOSE YOU AS A FRIEND.

PFFFT!

IT'D TAKE A LOT MORE THAN THAT TO LOSE ME.

OUR FRIENDSHIP IS STRONGER THAN A FEW ANGRY WORDS.

145

AND A MAGICAL TEMPER TANTRUM?

LISTEN, I'D TAKE THAT OVER THE BORING PONY YOU WERE BECOMING ANY DAY.

THE STARLIGHT I LOVE IS PASSIONATE, LIVELY...

...AND YEAH, SOMETIMES ANGRY.

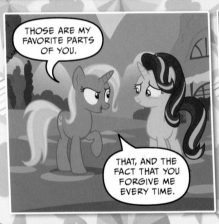

THOSE ARE MY FAVORITE PARTS OF YOU.

THAT, AND THE FACT THAT YOU FORGIVE ME EVERY TIME.

I'LL FORGIVE YOU IF YOU FORGIVE ME.

DEAL.

GAH!

I REMEMBER WHAT I WAS THINKING ABOUT!

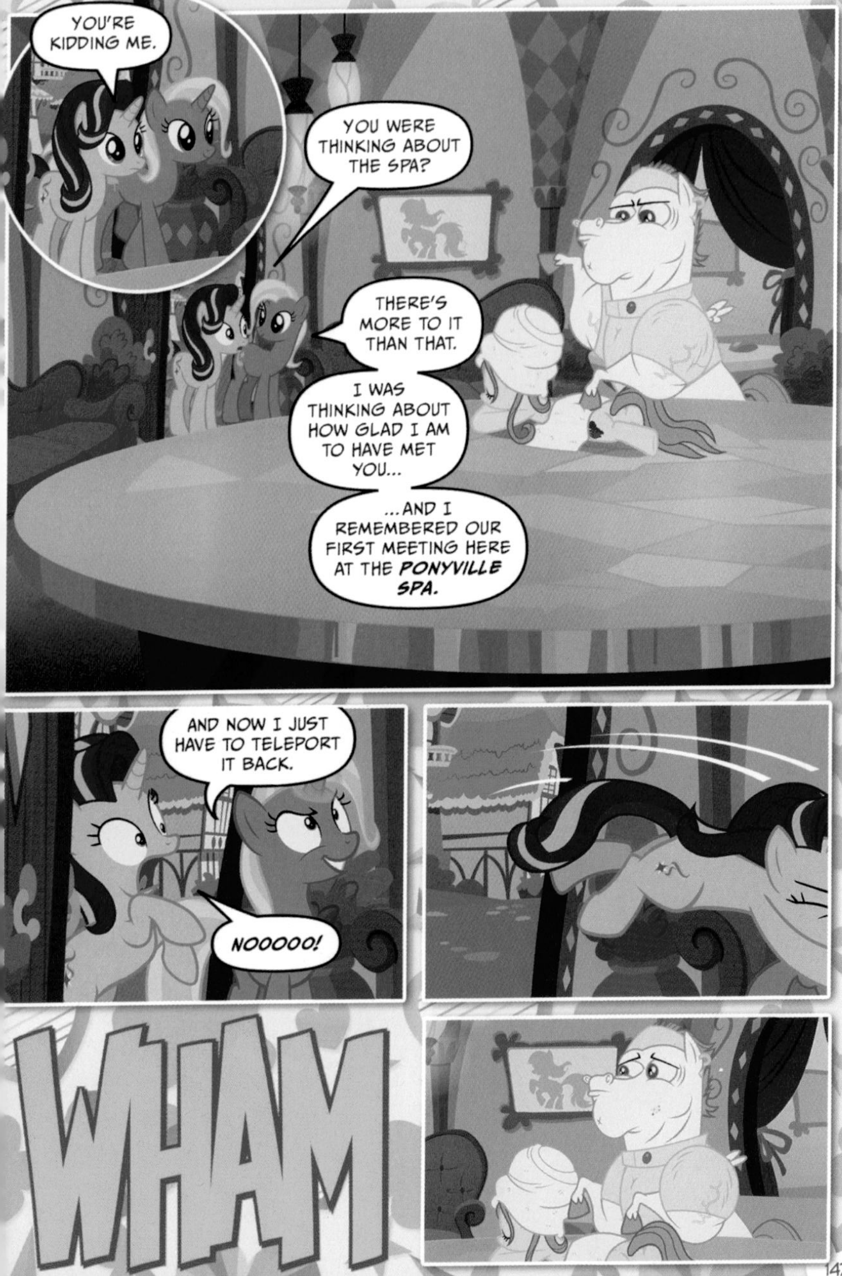
YOU'RE KIDDING ME.
YOU WERE THINKING ABOUT THE SPA?
THERE'S MORE TO IT THAN THAT.
I WAS THINKING ABOUT HOW GLAD I AM TO HAVE MET YOU...
...AND I REMEMBERED OUR FIRST MEETING HERE AT THE *PONYVILLE SPA.*
AND NOW I JUST HAVE TO TELEPORT IT BACK.
NOOOOO!
WHAM

A SHORT WHILE LATER...

VRRRNNN

A LITTLE TO THE LEFT...

NOW ROTATE IT *JUUUST* A HAIR—

HEY GIRLS! HOW DID IT GO?

THE MAP HITS THE FLOOR!

BAM

NOTHING!

WHAT?!

LET'S JUST SAY I LEARNED A FRIENDSHIP LESSON...

...WHILE YOU WERE GONE.

YOU'VE BARELY GRADUATED AND YOU'RE ALREADY TAKING INITIATIVE!

WE LEARNED ABOUT TEAM BUILDING, AND PROBLEM SOLVING—

WE CERTAINLY HAD A GOOD TIME...

...BUT I REALLY WAS LOOKING FORWARD TO A SPA DAY.

AND THE PONYVILLE SPA IS STILL OPEN.

ANYONE WANNA JOIN?

149

WE'LL MEET YOU THERE!

QUICK. DO YOU HAVE A SPELL...

...THAT WILL MAKE THE SPA PONIES FORGET THAT THE MAP TABLE WAS THERE?

HAVEN'T YOU LEARNED *ANYTHING* ABOUT USING MAGIC TO SOLVE YOUR PROBLEMS?

NO.

IF WE LEARN THAT LESSON...

...HOW WILL WE EVER HAVE FUN?

TEE-HEE

Not the End!

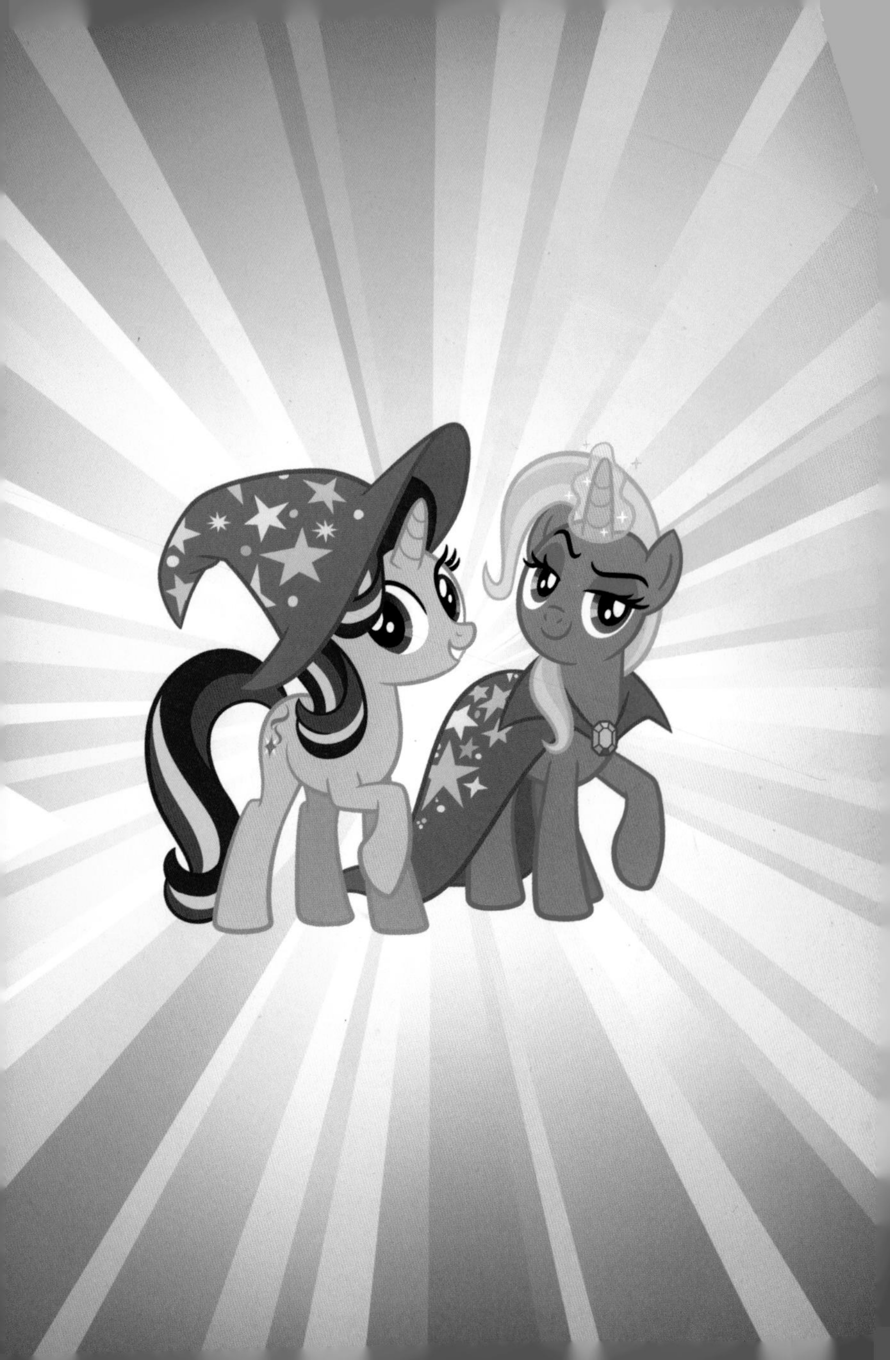

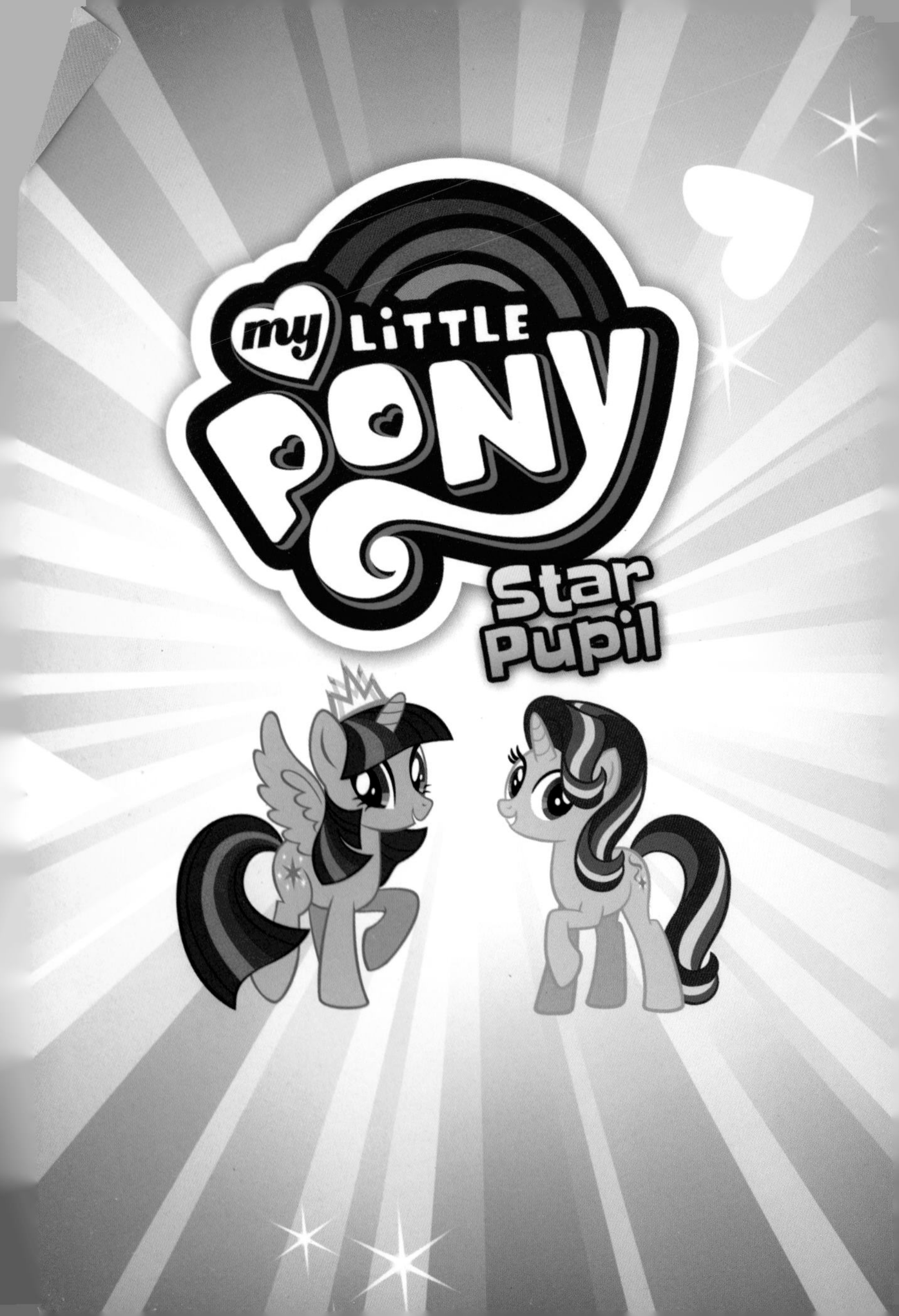
my LiTTLE PONY
Star Pupil